# MR. TOPSY-TURVY

by Roger Hargreaves

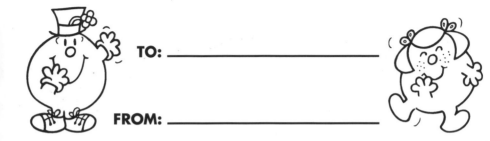

**TO:** _____

**FROM:** _____

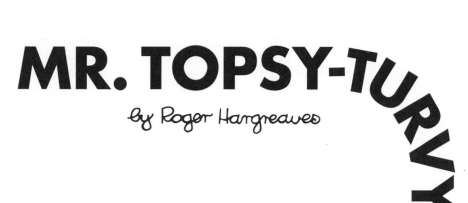

# MR. TOPSY-TURVY
### by Roger Hargreaves

Grosset & Dunlap

Mr. Topsy-Turvy was a funny sort of a fellow.

Everything about him was either upside-down, or inside out, or back to front—topsy-turvy, in fact.

It was all very extraordinary!

To give you some idea of how topsy-turvy
Mr. Topsy-Turvy was, you ought to see his house.

The front door is upside-down to start with.

And the curtains hang upside down at the windows.

And just look at that chimney!

All very extraordinary!

Inside it's just the same.

Just look at the clock standing on Mr. Topsy-Turvy's mantelpiece.

Isn't that the topsiest-turviest clock you've ever seen?

And just look at the way Mr. Topsy-Turvy reads a book.

Not only does he read it upside down, but he starts to read it at the back page!

Now, this story is all about the time Mr. Topsy-Turvy came to the town where you and I live.

Nobody is quite sure how Mr. Topsy-Turvy got there, or where he came from, but he did arrive, because somebody saw him getting off the train.

The trouble was, he did it in a topsy-turvy way, and got out the wrong side and fell onto the tracks.

Which really isn't all that surprising, is it?

When he'd picked himself up and managed to find his way out of the station, Mr. Topsy-Turvy went to a hotel to find a room to spend the night.

The hotel manager tried not to smile when he saw Mr. Topsy-Turvy walk into his hotel carrying his suitcase upside down and with his topsy-turvy hat on his head.

"Good afternoon, sir," he said. "Can I help you?"

Now, something you didn't know about Mr. Topsy-Turvy is the way he speaks.

You see, he sometimes gets things the wrong way round.

"Afternoon good," said Mr. Topsy-Turvy to the hotel manager. "I'd room a like!"

The manager scratched his head. "You mean you'd like a room?" he asked.

"Please yes," replied Mr. Topsy-Turvy.

Eventually the hotel manager managed to work out what Mr. Topsy-Turvy was talking about, and he was taken up in the elevator to a bedroom.

Then Mr. Topsy-Turvy unpacked his suitcase, put on his pajamas, and went to bed.

He was rather tired after traveling from wherever he'd come from.

The following day, Mr. Topsy-Turvy went round the town.

But what a fuss his going round the town caused.

He took a taxi from the hotel, but so confused the taxi driver trying to tell him where he wanted to go, the poor man drove straight into a traffic light.

"Oh dear," said Mr. Topsy-Turvy. "I am sorry very!"

Then he went into a big department store in the middle of the town.

He walked up to one of the counters.

"I'd like a sock of pairs," he said to the lady behind the counter.

"You mean a pair of socks," she smiled, and showed him a pair of bright red socks.

Mr. Topsy-Turvy put them on his hands!

Then he tried to leave, but being Mr. Topsy-Turvy he tried to walk down the up escalator, and all the people who were going up the up escalator all fell over themselves.

It was a terrible topsy-turvy jumble!

He went to a library and put all the books upside down on the shelves, and made everybody extremely angry.

Then he went to an art gallery and insisted on hanging all the pictures upside down so that he could look at them properly.

And then, after Mr. Topsy-Turvy had been in the town for just one day, he disappeared.

Nobody knew how he went, or where he went, but he certainly went because he wasn't there anymore.

The whole town breathed a sigh of relief.

But . . .

What the town discovered, even though
Mr. Topsy-Turvy had left, was that everything
was still topsy-turvy.

"News the is here," shouted the newscasters,
instead of saying, "Here is the news."

"Morning good," people started saying to each
other when they met, and "Do do you how?"
instead of "How do you do?"

Everybody was talking topsy-turvy!

Can you think of something to say that's topsy-turvy?

Go on, try!

**MR. MEN     LITTLE MISS**
*by Roger Hargreaves*

GROSSET & DUNLAP
An Imprint of Penguin Random House LLC, New York

Visit us online at www.penguinrandomhouse.com.

www.mrmen.com

ISBN 9780843176544                                          1 0 9 8

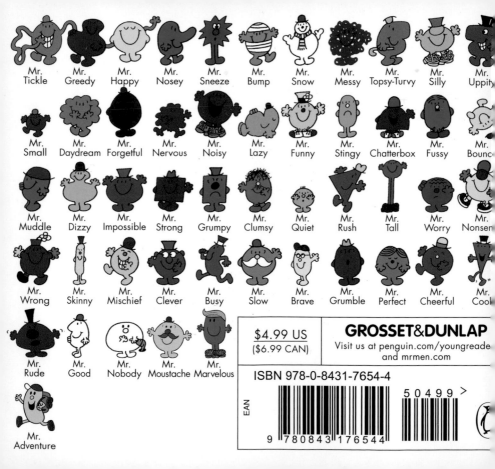

Mr. Tickle
Mr. Greedy
Mr. Happy
Mr. Nosey
Mr. Sneeze
Mr. Bump
Mr. Snow
Mr. Messy
Mr. Topsy-Turvy
Mr. Silly
Mr. Uppity

Mr. Small
Mr. Daydream
Mr. Forgetful
Mr. Nervous
Mr. Noisy
Mr. Lazy
Mr. Funny
Mr. Stingy
Mr. Chatterbox
Mr. Fussy
Mr. Bounce

Mr. Muddle
Mr. Dizzy
Mr. Impossible
Mr. Strong
Mr. Grumpy
Mr. Clumsy
Mr. Quiet
Mr. Rush
Mr. Tall
Mr. Worry
Mr. Nonsense

Mr. Wrong
Mr. Skinny
Mr. Mischief
Mr. Clever
Mr. Busy
Mr. Slow
Mr. Brave
Mr. Grumble
Mr. Perfect
Mr. Cheerful
Mr. Cool

Mr. Rude
Mr. Good
Mr. Nobody
Mr. Moustache
Mr. Marvelous

Mr. Adventure

$4.99 US
($6.99 CAN)

GROSSET&DUNLAP
Visit us at penguin.com/youngreade
and mrmen.com

ISBN 978-0-8431-7654-4

EAN

9 780843 176544

50499 >